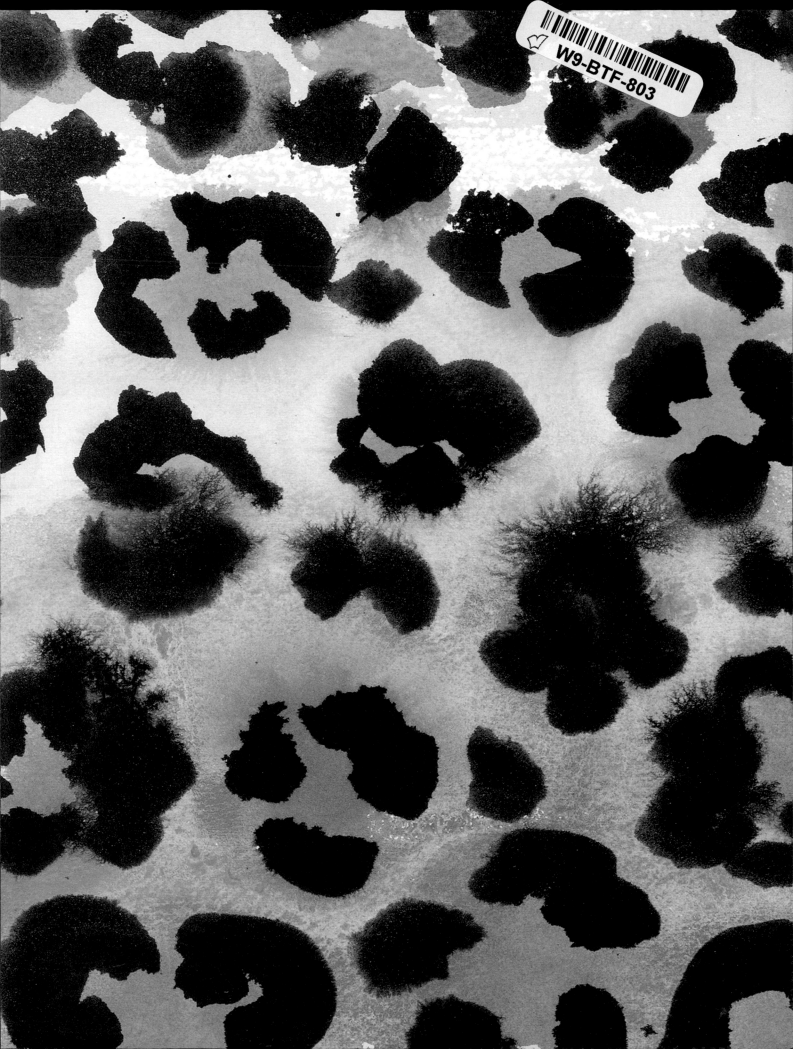

THE BEAUTY OF THE BEAST

POEMS FROM THE ANIMAL KINGDOM

selected by

Jack Prelutsky

illustrated by

Meilo So

*Opening poems for each section especially written
for this anthology by Jack Prelutsky.*

ALFRED A. KNOPF
New York

For Millicent and David-Paul

— J. P.

To Lamma Island

— M. S.

THIS IS A BORZOI BOOK PUBLISHED BY ALFRED A. KNOPF, INC.

Compilation copyright © 1997 by Jack Prelutsky

"In Trillions We Thrive," "Jubilant, We Swim," "Dragons in Miniature," "Hollow-Boned Singers,"

and "Wrapped in Coats of Fur" copyright © 1997 by Jack Prelutsky

Illustrations copyright © 1997 by Meilo So

Jacket hand-lettering by Bernard Maisner

Published in the United States by Alfred A. Knopf, Inc., New York, and simultaneously in Canada

by Random House of Canada Limited, Toronto. Distributed by Random House, Inc., New York.

Acknowledgments for permission to reprint previously published

material can be found on pages 99–101.

http://www.randomhouse.com/

Library of Congress Cataloging-in-Publication Data

The Beauty of the Beast : poems / selected by Jack Prelutsky ; illustrated by Meilo So.

p.   cm.

Includes bibliographical references and index.

Summary: An illustrated collection of poems about animals, insects,

and birds by poets from different parts of the world.

ISBN 0-679-87058-X (trade) — ISBN 0-679-97058-4 (lib. bdg.)

1. Animals—Juvenile poetry. 2. Children's poetry. [1. Animals—Poetry. 2. Poetry—Collections.]

I. Prelutsky, Jack.

II. So, Meilo, ill.

PN6110.A7B43   1997

811.008'036—dc20

96-14423

Printed in the United States of America 10 9 8 7 6 5 4 3 2 1

CONTENTS

In Trillions We Thrive

In trillions we thrive,
Cased in exoskeletons—
Ubiquitous motes.

ANT

The ant walks around
and upside down
carrying his weight ten times.

Fifty times his height the wall
he scales in three seconds—
over in a flash.

He buffets into high grasses
crashes through a dewy web
goes in a circle—heads
the wrong way—drops
the weight—picks it up
finds his path home—
hands it over:
a festival in the tunnels.

BARRY WALLENSTEIN

THE ANTS CRAWL

The ants crawl
over my arm
and back
into the grass
again.

They mean me
no harm.

I am only a
mountain
to them.

ELEANOR SCHICK

2

ANT

Black is his color
And he comes out of darkness
To a space of light
Where the grass rattles
And the wind booms.

In his home underground
The stones are silent
Roots and seeds make no noise.

Like fine wires
His legs tremble
Over the ground.

Raindrops hiss and explode
Around him
But he runs zig-zagging
From their cold touch.

At last one raindrop,
Bright balloon of water,
Bursts on his back
Becoming his own flood.
Frantic, he spins,
Finds ground again, and scurries
Towards some crack in an enormous Ark.

ZOË BAILEY

RAIN

Rain
bends
the tall grass
making
bridges
for ant.

JOANNE RYDER

THE GNATS

The gnats are dancing in the sun,
In vibrant needles of light they run
On the air, and hover in noiseless sound,
Ecstasy ballet, round and around,
Soon for human body bound.

The pin-thin slivers, wingy, white,
Whirl in restless, passionate flight—
Zooming atoms circling, twisting,
Darting, jiving,
Target-diving.
In orbit on orbit of dazzle-gold light,
The gnats are limbering up to bite.

ODETTE TCHERNINE

OH THE TOE-TEST!

The fly, the fly,
in the wink of an eye,
can taste with his feet
if the syrup is sweet
or the bacon is salty.
Oh is it his fault he
gets toast on his toes
as he tastes as he goes?

NORMA FARBER

MOSQUITO

There is more
To a mosquito
Than her sting
Or the way she sings
In the ear:

There are her wings
As clear
As windows,
There are the sleek
Velvets on her back;

She bends six
Slender knees,
And her eye, that
Sees the swatter,
Glitters.

VALERIE WORTH

4

THE GRASSHOPPER

Grasshopper
grasshopper
all day long
we hear your scraping
summer song
    like
        rusty
            fiddles
                in
            the
            grass
as through
        the meadow
            path
                we pass
such funny legs
such funny feet
and how we wonder
what you eat
maybe a single blink of dew
sipped from a clover leaf would do
then high in air
        once more you spring
            to fall in grass again
                and sing.

CONRAD AIKEN

SPLINTER

The voice of the last cricket
across the first frost
is one kind of good-bye.
It is so thin a splinter of singing.

CARL SANDBURG

THE GRASSHOPPER SPRINGS

The grasshopper springs,
    and catches the summer wind
        with his outstretched wings.

JAMES W. HACKETT

5

BUMBLE BEE

Black and yellow
Little fur bee
Buzzing away
In the timothy
Drowsy
Browsy
Lump of a bee
Rumbly
Tumbly
Bumbly bee.
Where are you taking
Your golden plunder
Humming along
Like baby thunder?
Over the clover
And over the hay
Then over the apple trees
Zoom away.

MARGARET WISE BROWN

BEE SONG

Bees in the late summer sun
Drone their song
Of yellow moons
Trimming black velvet,
Droning, droning a sleepysong.

CARL SANDBURG

THE FIRST WASP

Of all the plagues that heaven has sent,
A wasp is most impertinent.

JOHN GAY

WASP

Like a dark
Flame flickering
At the puddle's
Muddy rim,

Gathering a single
Dab, gone,
Glittering back
For more,

She is sprightly
And dangerous
In her ornamental
Blue-black bone,

She is a sharp
Flake of night
Let loose
In daylight,

A dab of dark
Earth, grown
Lively and deadly
As the sun.

VALERIE WORTH

THE WASP

Where the ripe pears droop heavily
    The yellow wasp hums loud and long
    His hot and drowsy autumn song:
A yellow flame he seems to be,
    When darting suddenly from high
    He lights where fallen peaches lie:
Yellow and black, this tiny thing's
A tiger soul on elfin wings.

WILLIAM SHARP

SUMMER

Wait!
I hear a knocking on the grass
Where dragon-visaged caterpillars pass.
They lean against grass stalks and sigh.
Their thoughts, like clouds of beetles,
Fill the air.
The cricket-crackling of their mandibles
Grates on the night.
I wait. No light from firefly or moth
Disturbs their eating.
Leaf after leaf descends the dragon maw.
I smooth my hand across the sheet and sigh.
The summer night crawls by.

PATRICIA HUBBELL

BUTTERFLIES

Fallen petals rise
    back to the branch—I watch:
        oh . . . butterflies!

MORITAKE

COCOON

The little caterpillar creeps
Awhile before in silk it sleeps.
It sleeps awhile before it flies,
And flies awhile before it dies,
And that's the end of three good tries.

DAVID McCORD

CATERPILLARS

They came like dewdrops overnight
Eating every plant in sight,
Those nasty worms with legs that crawl
So creepy up the garden wall,
Green prickly fuzz to hurt and sting
Each unsuspecting living thing.
How I hate them! Oh, you know
I'd love to squish them with my toe.
But then I see past their disguise,
Someday they'll all be butterflies.

BROD BAGERT

TO A MONARCH BUTTERFLY

Traveling jewel of the skies,
Orange-hued and black.
How gracefully you flit about
My garden, front and back.

You feed on nectar of the flowers,
At night you rest on trees,
Tiny airborne travelers—
You're filled with mysteries.

You seem so frail and delicate,
A breeze can waft you near.
You're filled with boundless energy…
I reach, you disappear!

And I am left with memories,
Exquisite, rare, apart…
Until the day that you return
I'll remember nature's art.

LOLA SNEYD

BLUE-BUTTERFLY DAY

It is blue-butterfly day here in spring,
And with these sky-flakes down in flurry
    on flurry
There is more unmixed color on the wing
Than flowers will show for days unless
    they hurry.

But these are flowers that fly and all but
    sing:
And now from having ridden out desire
They lie closed over in the wind and cling
Where wheels have freshly sliced the
    April mire.

ROBERT FROST

9

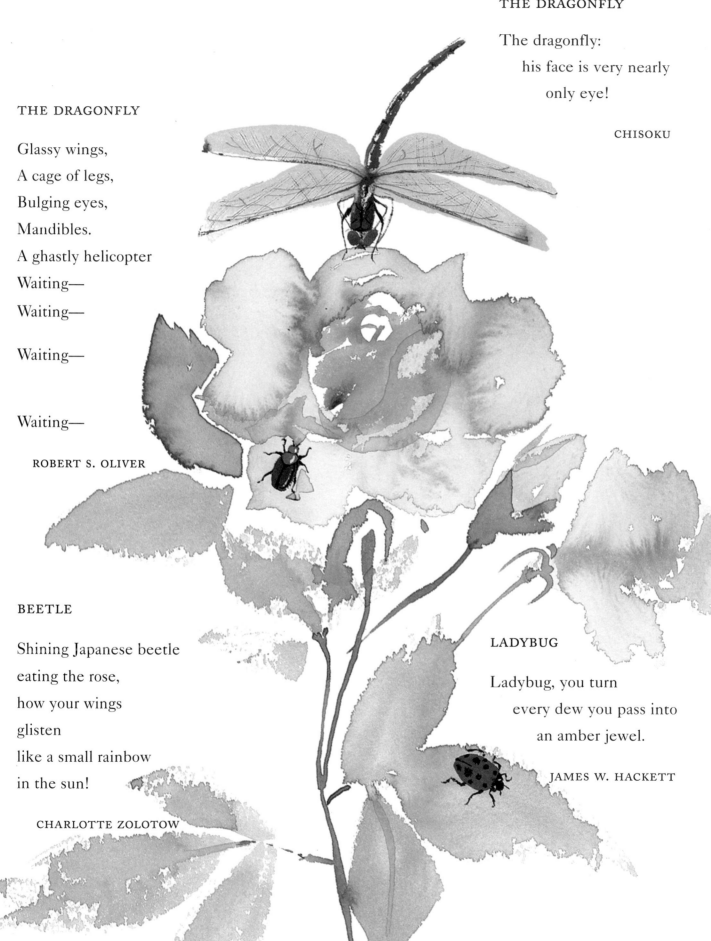

THE DRAGONFLY

The dragonfly:
    his face is very nearly
        only eye!

CHISOKU

THE DRAGONFLY

Glassy wings,
A cage of legs,
Bulging eyes,
Mandibles.
A ghastly helicopter
Waiting—

Waiting—

Waiting—

Waiting—

ROBERT S. OLIVER

BEETLE

Shining Japanese beetle
eating the rose,
how your wings
glisten
like a small rainbow
in the sun!

CHARLOTTE ZOLOTOW

LADYBUG

Ladybug, you turn
    every dew you pass into
        an amber jewel.

JAMES W. HACKETT

I CATCH A FIREFLY

I catch a firefly
    In cupped hands. My fingers glow
With imprisoned fire.

REBECCA CAUDILL

THE MOTH AND THE LAMP

The moth,
Enraged,
Beats against the lamp,
His wings forming
Countless tiny fans,
And falls at last
A fragile pinch of gray ashes.
The lamp burns on,
Tranquilly.

PAUL ELDRIDGE

NIGHT SONG

When the sun has set
And night has come,
The insect chorus
Starts to hum.

And nothing else
Is there to hear,
But the insect voices
Soft and clear.

FIREFLIES IN THE GARDEN

Here come real stars to fill the upper skies,
And here on earth come emulating flies,
That though they never equal stars in size,
(And they were never really stars at heart)
Achieve at times a very star-like start.
Only, of course, they can't sustain the part.

The insects hum
In sweet delight,
Singing their praises
Of the night.

ROBERT FROST

LELAND B. JACOBS

THE EARTHWORM WRIGGLES

The earthworm wriggles
   in confusion, but his head
     knows where it's going.

JAMES W. HACKETT

OH, TO BE AN EARTHWORM

Oh, to be an earthworm.
It has five hearts.
When one is pained or pierced
the other four carry on.
It has no chin to "take it" on,
no upper lip, no backbone
to keep stiff, just crawls
along in closest touch with earth;
doesn't yearn at the stars
or stretch for the moon
but goes about its intimate
business, living its soft life
to the full, savoring it
inch by inch.

LILLIAN MORRISON

THE CENTIPEDE

I objurgate the centipede,
A bug we do not really need.
At sleepy-time he beats a path
Straight to the bedroom or the bath.
You always wallop where he's not,
Or, if he is, he makes a spot.

OGDEN NASH

THE SNAIL

At sunset, when the night-dews fall,
Out of the ivy on the wall
With horns outstretched and pointed tail
Comes the gray and noiseless snail.
On ivy stems she clambers down,
Carrying her house of brown.
Safe in the dark, no greedy eye
Can her tender body spy,
While she herself, a hungry thief,
Searches out the freshest leaf.
She travels on as best she can
Like a toppling caravan.

JAMES REEVES

A SPIDER DOESN'T FLY

A spider doesn't fly
but walks off the edge of a beam
and waits for a bump
where all eight feet will feel firm
    dirt again
and all that silk slack between
will float off till it meets with
the last flakes off the last specks
spinning through the blue.

MICHAEL ROSEN

THE SPIDER

The spider, sly and talented,
weaves silver webs of silken thread,
then waits for unobservant flies
. . . to whom she'll not apologize!

JACK PRELUTSKY

DADDYLONGLEGS

Daddylonglegs need not worry
If he's ever in a hurry
And must leave a leg behind;
Daddylonglegs need not mind.
Even if he does not find it,
Daddylonglegs need not mind it;
He will quickly grow another.
So will Daddylonglegs' mother
And his sister and his brother
Also known as Daddylonglegs;
They will all grow brand-new strong legs.
Meanwhile, till the eighth they add,
Seven legs will do for Dad.

MARY ANN HOBERMAN

14

Jubilant, We Swim

Our sleek silver world
Ebbs and flows . . . mysterious.
Jubilant, we swim.

TROUT

Hangs, a fat gun-barrel,
deep under arched bridges
or slips like butter down
the throat of the river.

From the depths smooth-skinned as plums
his muzzle gets bull's eye;
picks off grass-seed and moths
that vanish, torpedoed.

Where water unravels
over gravel-bed he
is fired from the shallows
white belly reporting

flat; darts like a tracer-
bullet back between stones
and is never burnt out.
A volley of cold blood

ramrodding the current.

SEAMUS HEANEY

GOLDFISH

Hidden by the lily pots
Dark in the deeps
I hang softly
A thousand sleeps;
Born of the dim depths,
World as pool,
Gray-still, green-still,
Calming, cool;
Sunlight flecks
Glitter through heights
That scatter goldness
In shimmering sights.
Up to the surface, I
To the rain—
A moment's flash,
Then down again.

JOHN TRAVERS MOORE

CATFISH

The leopard eye of a murderer
and the body of an eel
combine to form a velvet glove
that has a grip like steel.

J. F. HENDRY

FISH

Look at them flit
Lickety-split
Wiggling
Swiggling
Swerving
Curving
Hurrying
Scurrying
Chasing
Racing
Whizzing
Whisking
Flying
Frisking
Tearing around
With a leap and a bound
But none of them making the tiniest
            tiniest
              tiniest
                tiniest
                  sound.

MARY ANN HOBERMAN

17

LITTLE FISH

The tiny fish enjoy themselves
in the sea.
Quick little splinters of life,
their little lives are fun to them
in the sea.

D. H. LAWRENCE

THE FISH'S WARNING

Stay by the water, stand on your shadow, stare
At my quick gliding, my darting body. You're made of air
And I of water. I do not know if you mean to throw
Your line, I move very fast, swim with fins much quicker
Than your thin arms. Rushes will hide me and will
Darken me. I'm a pulse of silver, something the moon
    tossed down.
I am frail for your finding but one whom only the night
    can drown.

ELIZABETH JENNINGS

THE ANCIENT BASS

Long and black and swift and narrow
As the shadow of an arrow,
Back and forth the old bass shoots
Down among the lily roots.

GRACE TABER HALLOCK

THE SHARK

My dear, let me tell you about the shark.

Though his eyes are bright, his thought is dark.

He's quiet—that speaks well of him.

So does the fact that he can swim.

But though he swims without a sound,

Wherever he swims he looks around

With those two bright eyes and that one dark thought.

He has only one but he thinks it a lot.

And the thought he thinks but can never complete

Is his long dark thought of something to eat.

Most anything does. And I have to add

That when he eats his manners are bad.

He's a gulper, a ripper, a snatcher, a grabber.

Yes, his manners are drab. But his thought is drabber.

That one dark thought he can never complete

Of something—anything—somehow to eat.

Be careful where you swim, my sweet.

JOHN CIARDI

SONG OF THE SILVER FISH

Little fishes in the sea
Swish your silver tails to lee,
Mind the blubber whale and shark,
Never swim far after dark.
In the darkness of the sea,
All the sunlight you can see
Is the waving pale green light
From a sun that's out of sight.
Moonfish, sunfish, starfish, ray
Take no sunlight from the day,
Sun and moon are far away.

MARGARET WISE BROWN

LOVE SONG FOR A JELLYFISH

How amazed I was, when I was a child,
To see your life on the sand.
To see you living in your jelly shape,
Round and slippery and dangerous.
You seemed to have fallen
Not from the rim of the sea,
But from the galaxies.
Stranger, you delighted me. Weird object of
The stinging world.

SANDRA HOCHMAN

A JELLYFISH

Visible, invisible,
      a fluctuating charm
an amber-tinctured amethyst
      inhabits it, your arm
approaches and it opens
      and it closes; you had meant
to catch it and it quivers;
      you abandon your intent.

MARIANNE MOORE

THE EEL

The feel
Of an eel
Is slippery,
Slimy;
He's sleek
And he's black
As a panther
At night.
He slides
Through your fingers
Rapidly,
Slyly;
A flip
Of his tail
And he slips
Out of sight.

ROBERT S. OLIVER

THOUGHTS ABOUT OYSTERS

An oyster has no hands or feet
To put itself in motion.
It never waves or runs to meet
Companions in the ocean.

It has no mouth or nose or eyes
Like other water creatures,
Which makes it hard to recognize
An oyster by its features.

An oyster can't go any place.
It huddles in its shell;
And, though it hasn't got a face,
I guess it's just as well.

An oyster's personality
Is dull beyond expression;
And meeting oysters suddenly
You get a poor impression.

The gayest oyster never spends
Its time in fun or roistering,
Which means an oyster's only friends
Are people who go oystering.

The people greet it with a knife
And lemon juice—and therefore
I often think an oyster's life
Is not a life I'd care for.

KAYE STARBIRD

CRAB

All his savings are sunk in his claws.
Like frightened roots sprung out of his head
His eyes pop out on everlasting stilts.
When he walks, he is a six-legged plant,
Fortifications on top, and rock back,
Supplies safeguarded, a real crab.

J. F. HENDRY

OCTOPUS

Marvel at the
Awful many-armed
Sea-god Octopus,
And the coiled
Elbows of his eager
Eightfold embrace;

Yet also at his
Tapered tender
Fingertips, ferrying
Their great brow
Along the sea floor
In solitary grace.

VALERIE WORTH

21

CRAB DANCE

Play moonlight
and the red crabs dance
their scuttle-foot dance
on the mud-packed beach

Play moonlight
and the red crabs dance
their sideways dance
to the soft-sea beat

Play moonlight
and the red crabs dance
their bulb-eye dance
their last crab dance

GRACE NICHOLS

Dragons in Miniature

Winders and sliders,
Dragons in miniature,
Our life blood runs cold.

THE TORTOISE

The tortoise has a tendency
To live beyond his prime,
Thus letting his descendants see
How *they* will look in time.

COLIN WEST

MUD TURTLES

On the rock the turtles get
When they are tired of being wet.
Back into the pond they slide
When they are tired of being dried.

GRACE TABER HALLOCK

LIVING TENDERLY

My body a rounded stone
with a pattern of smooth seams.
My head a short snake,
retractive, projective.
My legs come out of their sleeves
or shrink within,
and so does my chin.
My eyelids are quick clamps.

My back is my roof.
I am always at home.
I travel where my house walks.
It is a smooth stone.
It floats within the lake,
or rests in the dust.
My flesh lives tenderly
inside its bone.

MAY SWENSON

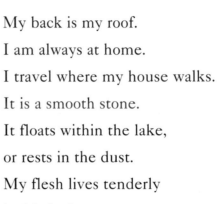

SO BUSY

So busy
watching a fly,
small turtle
does not see
night come.

The sun
and the pond
disappear.
Over so soon,
she sighs,
and tucks herself
inside the darkness
she will
always call
home.

JOANNE RYDER

NAMING THE TURTLE

Slowpod,
Weightlifter,
Housemover,
Homelover.

Seaflipper,
Rainstopper,
Pond-land-
 and-stream-dweller.

Platepacker,
Boneback,
Hardshell
and Softhat.

Clicktoe
and Stare-eye,
Budhead
and Stemneck.

Nob-bob and
Lookslow,
Spotback
and Ridgetop.

Plod-plod
and Plopplop,

Logloving
Rockstone.

PATRICIA HUBBELL

TURTLE TIME

My time is
slow time,
old time,

the unhurried
time of
turtles
long ago.

Slowly,
I make my way.

Why hurry?

There was turtle time
before there was
people time.

LILIAN MOORE

A LAZY LIZARD

A lazy lizard lying
on a sunny granite ledge,
stretches out its lazy toes
until they touch the edge.

Then it flits its lazy tongue
to catch a morning munch,
a crunch to quell its appetite
until its lazy lunch.

It flips upon its lazy back
and then it flops on top.
For even lizards know how much
to sun and when to stop!

MICHELE KRUEGER

THE AXOLOTL

The axolotl acts a little
Fishily at times.
In Mexico, some gills he'll grow,
But when in cooler climes,
Upon dry land a salamander
He may choose to be,
Though why he should and how he could
Is still not clear to me!

COLIN WEST

RICH LIZARD

The rich lizard
shed his skin
of silver coins,
dropping them
in the dry grass.
Strange-wild thoughts
shook him,
warming his blood
to grander things,
and he tore himself
loose—
ran off,
leaving behind
his wealth of cold coins.

DEBORAH CHANDRA

THE SPADE-FOOT TOAD

The Spade-Foot Toad lives underground
And sits and waits, but makes no sound.
Above his head is burning sand—
For ten long months that Toad is canned!

He can't come out until it rains—
The blazing sun would bake his brains.
He counts the days, he counts the hours,
He waits for summer, with its showers,

And if—some day—all records broke
And no rain came, that Toad would croak!

EVE GANSON

THE TREE TOADS

Down by the old swamp road
The Tree Toads are quarreling
With cracked, insistent voices.
They have crept out to squat
By their little rooty doorways,
Under their lichen eaves,
For their nightly arguments
About the world in general—
And Tree Toads in particular.

RACHEL FIELD

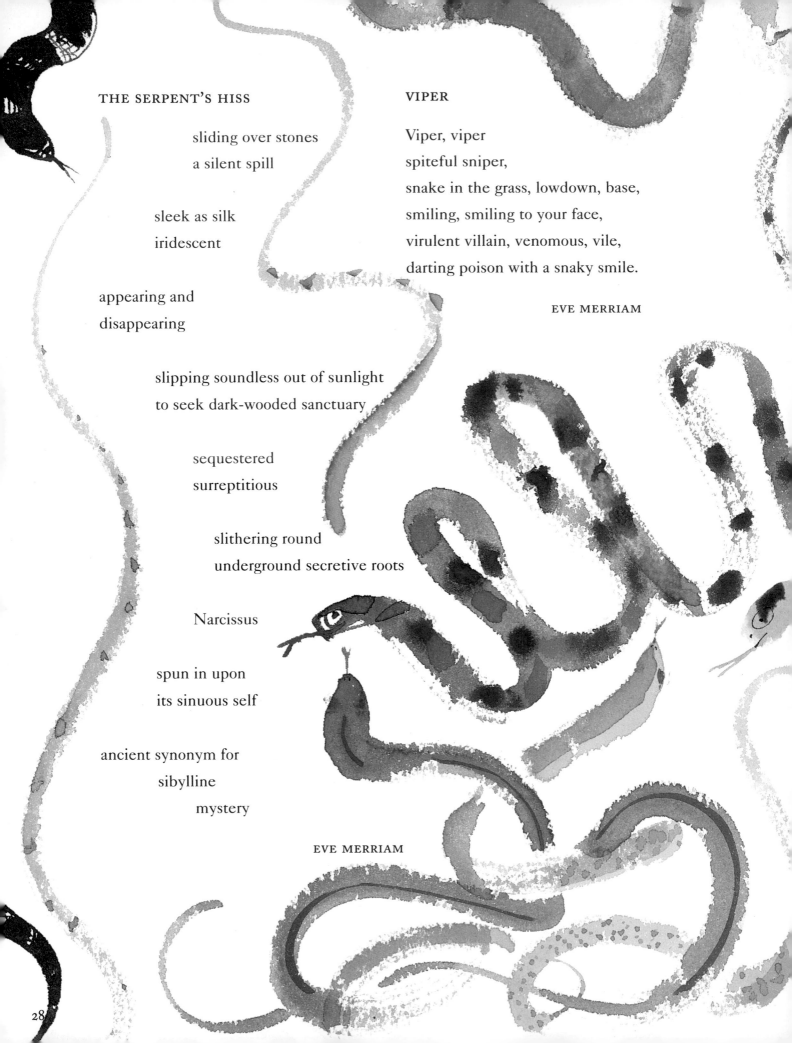

THE SERPENT'S HISS

sliding over stones
a silent spill

sleek as silk
iridescent

appearing and
disappearing

slipping soundless out of sunlight
to seek dark-wooded sanctuary

sequestered
surreptitious

slithering round
underground secretive roots

Narcissus

spun in upon
its sinuous self

ancient synonym for
sibylline
mystery

EVE MERRIAM

VIPER

Viper, viper
spiteful sniper,
snake in the grass, lowdown, base,
smiling, smiling to your face,
virulent villain, venomous, vile,
darting poison with a snaky smile.

EVE MERRIAM

28

I AM A SNAKE

I am a snake.
I snake alone
Through rushes and bushes
Past moss and stone.
I slide through grass,
The slim stalks sigh,
Bees buzz the news
As I slip by.
Mushrooms tremble,
Clover tumbles,
One slight field mouse squeaks
And stumbles.
Butterflies and bees and bumbles
Wing away to nests and hives,
Beetles scatter for their lives.
Silence settles where I wend.
The snake is slow to make a friend.

KARLA KUSKIN

SNAKE

I, the reptilian,
serpentine, jewel-eyed,
golden-scaled, spiraling
splendor of Snake,
I in the shallows of
Nigers and Amazons
I dream of Death
when I sleep, when I wake.
I bind the Bird and
the Beast and
all creatures in
my coiled fascination
no Lion could break.

I am the Python,
the Great Anaconda,
I am the Cobra the
King of Golconda,
I am the Winged, the
Plumed Aztec Serpent,

I am the Rainbow
that climbs in the tree,
I am the Kiss of Death,
the hiss of Darkness.
I and I only
do not fear me.

GEORGE BARKER

RATTLESNAKE

I move so flat against
the earth
that I know all
its mysteries.

I understand
the way sun
clings to rocks
after the sun is gone.

I understand
the long cold shadows
that wrap themselves
around me
and slow my blood
and call me back
into the earth.

On the south side of
a rocky slope
where sun can warm
my hiding place,
I wait for the cold
that draws me into
sleep.

I understand
waking
in spring,
still cold,

hardly moving,
seeking warmth,
seeking food,
going from darkness
to light.

I understand
the shedding
of old skin
and the tenderness
of my new soft shining
self
flowing
smooth as water
over sand.

I understand
the sudden strike,
the death I hold
behind my fangs.

Wherever I go
I cast
a shadow of fear.

BYRD BAYLOR

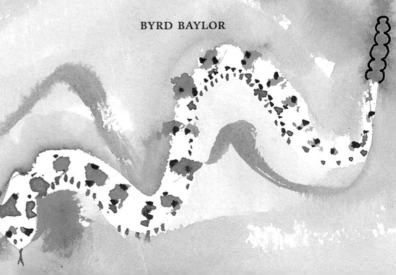

ALLIGATOR

Old bull of the waters,
old dinosaur cousin,
with scales by the hundreds
and teeth by the dozen,

old singer of swamp lands,
old slithery swimmer,
what do you dream of
when fireflies glimmer?

Can you remember
the folk tales of old
when you breathed fire
and guarded the gold

and stole lovely ladies
and captured their kings
and flew over mountains
on magical wings?

Old bull of the waters,
how can you know
men made you a dragon
in dreams, long ago?

MAXINE W. KUMIN

THE CROCODILE

This is a Crocodile, my boy…
Or is it an Alligator?…
I've an excellent book that you'll enjoy
We can refer to later;

The Alligator…no, Crocodile
Is a purplish color beneath.
Give it a tickle to make it smile
And let's count the number of teeth,

For the Croc (I think) has a row too few
Though the Gator can't wink its eye…

Ah!
    Now I can tell you which of the two
You have just been eaten by.

MICHAEL FLANDERS

31

FROGS IN SPRING

Maybe they're glad
for the warmth of spring—
that's why frogs
in the frog pond sing.

Maybe they're glad
to jump and leap
after their long cold
winter sleep.

Maybe they're glad
to see their friends—
that's why they sing
when winter ends.

Maybe they're glad
to *eat* once more.
That's what *I*
would be gladdest for.

AILEEN FISHER

FROG

Pollywiggle
Pollywog
Tadpole
Bullfrog
Leaps on
Long legs
Jug–o–rum
Jelly eggs
Sticky tongue
Tricks flies
Spied by
Flicker eyes
Wet skin
Cold blood
Squats in
Mucky mud
Leaps on
Long legs
Jug–o–rum
Jelly eggs
Laid in
Wet bog....
Pollywiggle
Pollywog.

MARY ANN HOBERMAN

32

Hollow-Boned Singers

Hollow-boned singers
Descended from dinosaurs,
The sky is our home.

CROWS

I like to walk
And hear the black crows talk.

I like to lie
And watch crows sail the sky.

I like the crow
That wants the wind to blow:

I like the one
That thinks the wind is fun.

I like to see
Crows spilling from a tree,

And try to find
The top crow left behind.

I like to hear
Crows caw that spring is near.

I like the great
Wild clamor of crow hate

Three farms away
When owls are out by day.

I like the slow
Tired homeward-flying crow;

I like the sight
Of crows for my good night.

DAVID McCORD

TEN BILLION CROWS

Ten billion crows with cracking bills
Ate all the corn off our eight hills.

Then round and round the sky they
   soared
And crowed and cruised, and snoozed and
   snored.

Dad said, "Well, that's the way it goes,
All that fine corn inside those crows."

I hope their bellies ache for weeks.
I hope they crash and break their beaks.

X. J. KENNEDY

DUST OF SNOW

The way a crow
Shook down on me
The dust of snow
From a hemlock tree

Has given my heart
A change of mood
And saved some part
Of a day I had rued.

ROBERT FROST

35

HUMMING BIRD

The humming bird refuels
in mid-air from the hub
of a fuchsia flower.
Its belly is feathered white
as rapids; its eye
is smaller than a drop of tar.
A bodied moth, it beats
stopwatches into lethargy
with its wingstrokes.

Food it needs every fifteen
minutes. It has the metabolism
of a steam engine.
Its tiny claws are slight
as pared fingernail;
you could slip it with ease
into a breast pocket.
There it might lie, cowed
—or give you a second heart.

PAUL GROVES

SONG-THRUSH

Slug-slayer, snail-snatcher,
soprano turned percussionist,
mad drummer of the rock;
now executioner,
still center-stage,
beats out her dizzy solo
on execution block.

JUDITH NICHOLLS

36

THE NUTHATCH

The nuthatch, when it climbs a tree,
Creeps left and right diagonally.
That's odd, of course; but, odder still,
On coming back the way it went,
Once more on the diagonal,
It makes an upside-down descent.
"Who, who, who" it nasally sings,
Tail pointing up to higher things.

CHARLES NORMAN

CARDINAL

Red as a shout
he stamps himself
like a Chinese signature
on the clean snow
under the dark juniper tree
in the park.

He is a scarlet stroke
of ink
brushed in—
a feathered ending
to a poem about
snow.

In the whole city
pale and dusted with
snow
only his wings are ablaze
with poppies!

BARBARA JUSTER ESBENSEN

PIGEONS

They paddle with staccato feet
In powder-pools of sunlight,
Small blue busybodies—
Strutting like fat gentlemen
With hands clasped
Under their swallowtail coats;
And, as they stump about,
Their heads like tiny hammers
Tap at imaginary nails
In non-existent walls.
Elusive ghosts of sunshine
Slither down the green gloss
Of their necks an instant, and are gone.

Summer hangs drugged from sky to earth
In limpid fathoms of silence:
Only warm dark dimples of sound
Slide like slow bubbles
From the contented throats.

Raise a casual hand—
With one quick gust
They fountain into air.

RICHARD KELL

WOODPECKER

Woodpecker is rubber-necked
    But has a nose of steel.
He bangs his head against the wall
    And cannot even feel.

When Woodpecker's jack-hammer head
    Starts up its dreadful din
Knocking the dead bough double dead
    How do his eyes stay in?

Pity the poor dead oak that cries
    In terrors and in pains.
But pity more Woodpecker's eyes
    And bouncing rubber brains.

TED HUGHES

PIGEONS

Pigeons are city folk
content
to live with concrete
and cement.

They seldom
try
the sky.

A pigeon never sings
of hill
and flowering hedge,
but busily commutes
from sidewalk
to his ledge.

Oh pigeon, what a waste of wings!

LILIAN MOORE

PIGEONS

A gray-blue pigeon
blows up his feathers
and struts
across the path
to other pigeons
waiting in the grass.
An old man
scatters breadcrumbs
and the pigeons
ripple up to his feet
in a blue and silver wave.

CHARLOTTE ZOLOTOW

SPARROW

Nothing is less
Rare than
One dust-
Colored sparrow
In a driveway
Minding her own
Matters, pottering
Carelessly, finding
Seeds in the tire-
Flattened weeds:

But because
She can dare
To let us watch her
There, when all
The stately robins
Have fled
Scolding into
The air, she
Is as good a bird
As anyone needs.

VALERIE WORTH

A BITTER MORNING

A bitter morning:
    sparrows sitting together
        without any necks.

JAMES W. HACKETT

39

IF I WERE A HAWK

If I were a hawk,
I would taste the tips of storm clouds
and clutch lightning bolts in my great claws.
I'd fold my wings and dive into forests
green as the Atlantic
with the wind polishing my feathers,
and then flap away again.

I'd fly through a hundred cloud-patched sunsets,
and hammer sungold to the pines with my curved beak.
I'd name the whole sky mine and call aloud to claim it,
circling the world till night eased me down on my nest.
An umbrella of stars over my shoulders,
I'd sleep without fear or nightmare in the dark
if I were a hawk.

                              MARY ANN COLEMAN

HARPY EAGLE

Hunger's keen eye slits the green
  canopy, flashes down leafy
    corridors, glints in dark
      chambers, fastens
        on a small
          warm
            m
             e
              a
               l

      ALICE SCHERTLE

THE SPARROW HAWK

Wings like pistols flashing at his sides,
Masked, above the meadow runway rides,
Galloping, galloping with an easy rein.
Below, the field mouse, where the shadow glides,
Holds fast the small purse of his life, and hides.

                      RUSSELL HOBAN

EAGLE

Big wings dawns dark.

The Sun is hunting.

Thunder collects, under granite eyebrows.

The horizons are ravenous.

The dark mountain has an electric eye.

The Sun lowers its meat-hook.

His spread fingers measure a heaven, then a heaven.

His ancestors worship only him,

And his children's children cry to him alone.

His trapeze is a continent.

The Sun is looking for fuel

With the gaze of a guillotine.

And already the White Hare crouches at the sacrifice,

Already the Fawn stumbles to offer itself up

And the Wolf-Cub weeps to be chosen.

The huddle-shawled lightning-faced warrior

Stamps his shaggy-trousered dance

On an altar of blood.

TED HUGHES

CLEANING

The owl has vacuumed
the wood again,
leaving two gray nubs
of dust again;
bone of shrew, mole, and bat,
rolled in their own
coughed-up fur.

ANN TURNER

THE BIRD OF NIGHT

A shadow is floating through the moonlight.
Its wings don't make a sound.
Its claws are long, its beak is bright.
Its eyes try all the corners of the night.

It calls and calls: all the air swells and heaves
And washes up and down like water.
The ear that listens to the owl believes
In death. The bat beneath the eaves,

The mouse beside the stone are still as death—
The owl's air washes them like water.
The owl goes back and forth inside the night,
And the night holds its breath.

RANDALL JARRELL

OWL

Owl
was darker
than ebony—
flew through the night
eyes like amber searchlights,
rested on a post,
feathers wind-ruffled,
stood stump still,
talons ready to seize
and squeeze.

Owl
was death
for it flew through the dark
that swamped the fields,
that tightened its knot,
that bandaged the hills
in a blindfold of fear.

Owl flew — Who — Who — Who —

PIE CORBETT

THE MULTILINGUAL MYNAH BIRD

Birds are known to cheep and chirp
and sing and warble, peep and purp,
and some can only squeak and squawk,
but the mynah bird is able to talk.

The mynah bird, the mynah bird,
a major, not a minor bird;
you'll never find a finer bird
than the multilingual mynah bird.

He can talk to you in Japanese,
Italian, French and Portuguese;
and even Russian and Chinese
the mynah bird will learn with ease.

The multilingual mynah bird
can say most any word he's heard,
and sometimes he invents a few
(a very difficult thing to do).

So if you want to buy a bird,
why don't you try the mynah bird?
You'll never find a finer bird
than the multilingual mynah bird.

JACK PRELUTSKY

44

I'M A PARROT

I am a parrot
I live in a cage
I'm nearly always
in a vex-up rage

I used to fly
all light and free
in the luscious green
forest canopy

I am a parrot
I live in a cage
I'm nearly always
in a vex-up rage

I miss the wind
against my wing
I miss the nut
and the fruit picking

I am a parrot
I live in a cage
I'm nearly always
in a vex-up rage

I squawk I talk
I curse I swear
I repeat the things
I shouldn't hear

So don't come near me
or put out your hand
because I'll pick you
if I can
pickyou
pickyou
if I can

I want to be Free
Can't You Understand

GRACE NICHOLS

45

PEACOCKS

A muster of peacocks
Where the sweetbrier trails:
I wish, and how I wish
They would open wide their tails,

Their tails spread like a fan
With scores of watching eyes,
Gold and blue and green,
Staring with surprise.

PAULINE CLARKE

BLUEBIRD

In the woods a piece of sky
fell down, a piece of blue.
"It must have come from very high,"
I said. "It looks so new."

It landed on a leafy tree
and there it seemed to cling,
and when I squinted up to see,
I saw it had a *wing*,

and then a *head*, and suddenly
I heard a bluebird sing!

AILEEN FISHER

46

TOUCANS

Picking fruit
isn't all
they're good for,
those boat beaks,
those blue and yellow
banana bills,
those pink and purple
splattered spatulas.

I have
seen you
ripping strips
of rainbow,
watched you
dragging the bright ribbons
through the branches
of the jungle trees.

ALICE SCHERTLE

STARLINGS

Like crumbs from someone's shaken tablecloth,
A score, at least, or more
Of speckled starlings drop upon the grass,
And seek, with nimble beak,
To snatch at every dainty that they pass.

They move in concert, picking as they go,
Precise, efficient, and concise;
Then weightless, effortless, lift, and fluttering fly,
A cloud of birds, into the cloudless sky.

LYDIA PENDER

THE REDBREAST

The redbreast smoulders in the waste of snow:
His eye is large and bright, and to and fro
He draws and draws his slender threads of sound
Between the dark boughs and the freezing ground.

ANTHONY RYE

47

PENGUIN

O Penguin, do you ever try
To flap your flipper wings and fly?
How do you feel, a bird by birth
And yet for life tied down to earth?
A feathered creature, born with wings
Yet never wing-borne. All your kings
And emperors must wonder why
Their realm is sea instead of sky.

MARY ANN HOBERMAN

EMPEROR PENGUINS

Huddled close together
Against the snow and sleet,
Penguins at the pole
Pool their body heat.

They gather in a circle,
Steadfast, disciplined,
Turning toward the center,
Fighting off the wind.

Sharing warmth and comfort
On cold and icy floes,
Balancing their future
Gently, on their toes.

AN AUK IN FLIGHT

An auk in flight
is sheer delight,
it soars above the sea.

An auk on land
is not so grand—
an auk walks **auk**wardly.

JACK PRELUTSKY

BARRY LOUIS POLISAR

GULL

Immobile.
Steel or painted wood
statue? Decoy?
Spreads sudden wings!
And can that heavy body lift
so
slow-
ly,
slow-
ly?
Then
crash-dive
into shallows,
beak grabbing
some sea creature,
then rising and
smashing it onto rocks.

       Diving
           again
to tear its living from a shell.

          FELICE HOLMAN

THE SANDPIPER

At the edge of tide
He stops to wonder,
Races through
The lace of thunder.

On toothpick legs
Swift and brittle,
He runs and pipes
And his voice is little.

But small or not,
He has a notion
To outshout
The Atlantic Ocean.

          FRANCES FROST

RUNIC BIRDS

Sandpiper steps
Imprint the sand:
Read backwards
In a line,
They seem to fly
Like runic birds
Beyond the shores
Of time.

          VICTORIA FORRESTER

EGRETS

Once as I traveled through a quiet evening,
I saw a pool, jet-black and mirror still.
Beyond, the slender paperbarks stood crowding;
each on its own white image looked its fill,
and nothing moved but thirty egrets wading—
thirty egrets in a quiet evening.

Once in a lifetime, lovely past believing,
your lucky eyes may light on such a pool.
As though for many years I had been waiting,
I watched in silence, till my heart was full
of clear dark water, and white trees unmoving,
and, whiter yet, those egrets wading.

JUDITH WRIGHT

THE HERON

The heron stands in water where the swamp
Has deepened to the blackness of a pool.
Or balances with one leg on a hump
Of marsh grass heaped above a muskrat hole.

He walks the shallow with an antic grace.
The great feet break the ridges of the sand.
The long eye notes the minnow's hiding place.
His beak is quicker than a human hand.

He jerks a frog across his bony lip.
Then points his heavy bill above the wood.
The wide wings flap but once to lift him up.
A single ripple starts from where he stood.

THEODORE ROETHKE

IBIS

There is a bird called the ibis…
it enjoys eating corpses or snakes' eggs,
and from such things it takes food home
for its young, which comes most acceptable.
It walks near the seashore by day and night,
looking for little dead fish or other bodies
which have been thrown up by the waves.
It is afraid to enter the water
because it cannot swim.

T. H. WHITE

THE SANDHILL CRANE

Whenever the days are cool and clear
The sandhill crane goes walking
Across the field by the flashing weir
Slowly, solemnly stalking.
The little frogs in the tules hear
And jump for their lives when he comes near,
The minnows scuttle away in fear,
When the sandhill crane goes walking.

The field folk know if he comes that way,
Slowly, solemnly stalking,
There is danger and death in the least delay
When the sandhill crane goes walking.
The chipmunks stop in the midst of their play,
The gophers hide in their holes away
And hush, oh, hush! the field mice say,
When the sandhill crane goes walking.

MARY AUSTIN

CRANE'S LEGS

Patiently the crane fishes in the lake,
His long red legs shortened since the rains.

BASHO

WILD GOOSE

He climbs the wind above
    green clouds of pine,
Honking to hail the
    gathering migration,
And, arching toward the
    south, pulls to align
His flight into the great
    spearhead formation.

He'll find a bayou land of
    hidden pools,
And bask amid lush fern
    and water lily
Far from the frozen world
    of earth-bound fools
Who, shivering, maintain
    that geese are silly.

CURTIS HEATH

A LONG FLAPPING V

A long flapping V
settles on the pond
honking
resting
eating the sweet grasses.

Their visit over,
the wild geese rise
climbing stairs
no one can see.

JOANNE RYDER

THE WILD GEESE RETURNING

The wild geese returning
Through the misty sky—
Behold they look like
A letter written
In faded ink!

TSUMORI KUNIMOTO

THE LOON

The Loon, the Loon
Hatched from the Moon

Writhes out of the lake
Like an airborne snake.

He swallows a trout
And then shakes out

A ghastly cry
As if the sky
Were trying to die.

TED HUGHES

SWANS IN THE NIGHT

Three swans
Under the moon,
Three shadows
On the lagoon.

Three swans
On the water ride,
Three shadows
Move beside.

Silver water,
Silent swans,
Swaying ferns
With silvered fronds.

A strolling cloud
Obscures the moon,
Gone the swans
From the dark lagoon.

JOAN MELLINGS

QUACK?

Quack sound is crisp,
Crackly-quick
As the snap of teeth
On a celery stick.
Do you think ducks
Ever feel absurd
Speaking a language of
Just one word?

MARY O'NEILL

CALLIGRAPHY

Duck.

                    Duck.
        Duck.

                    Duck.
Four mallards on a pond
write with the subtle
tracings of their backwash
a salutation to spring.

JANE YOLEN

THE CASSOWARY

Behold the scraggly cassowary
who is so very very *very*
hairy—and big—and see
his toes are three.
And why three?
Don't ask *me*.
And such legs
and such eggs
and that eye
that asks you *why?*
Why indeed have such a breed
and did we really *need?*
But then that very very
wary ancient cassowary
can say to us *you too*—
why *you?*
A question we had better beg
or eat the cassowary's egg.

CONRAD AIKEN

THE OSTRICH

His beak and skull are both so thick,
You could not hurt him with a brick.
His feet are large, his head is small,
He hasn't any brain at all.

ROLAND YOUNG

54

Wrapped in Coats of Fur

Four-legged marvels,
We range across the planet
Wrapped in coats of fur.

THE KANGAROO

It is a curious thing that you
don't wish to be a kangaroo,
    to hop hop hop
    and never stop
the whole day long and the whole night, too!

To hop across Australian plains
with tails that sweep behind like trains
    and small front paws
    and pointed jaws
and pale neat coats to shed the rains.

If skies be blue, if skies be gray,
they bound in the same graceful way
    into dim space
    at such a pace
that where they go there's none to say!

      ELIZABETH COATSWORTH

THE MOLE

One rarely gets to meet the mole,
He's such a misanthropic soul.
He tunnels blindly in the earth
And nothing knows of warmth or mirth.
A few close friends? No. Please excuse him—
Not even other moles amuse him.

JEANNE STEIG

THE RABBIT

When they said the time to hide was mine,
I hid back under a thick grape vine.

And while I was still for the time to pass,
A little gray thing came out of the grass.

He hopped his way through the melon bed
And sat down close by a cabbage head.

He sat down close where I could see,
And his big still eyes looked hard at me,

His big eyes bursting out of the rim,
And I looked back very hard at him.

ELIZABETH MADDOX ROBERTS

BEAVERS IN NOVEMBER

This stick here

That stick there

   Mud, more mud, add mud, good mud

That stick here

This stick there

   Mud, more mud, add mud, good mud

     You pat

     I gnaw

     I pile

     You store

This stick here

That stick there

  Mud, more mud, add mud, good mud

     You guard

     I pack

     I dig

     You stack

That stick here

This stick there

   Mud, more mud, add mud, good mud

     I trim

     You mold

     To keep

     Out cold

This stick here

That stick there

   Mud, more mud, add mud, good mud

MARILYN SINGER

ABOUT MUSKRAT, LET'S SAY . . .

You stroll along the stream

To where green rushes rise

And you stop beneath the willow

And there, to your surprise,

   A dome lies on the water,

Thatched of twigs and limbs and mud.

That's the roof of Muskrat's home.

But he's not there today, no—

He's decided he needs more;

One house is simply not enough…

So he's building him a second

From the stream into the shore.

That's why Muskrat's down-under now

Bubble-breathing, beaver-style.

He's tossing dirt like a digging machine

While treading water with his webbed hind feet

And not to be disturbed, but—

He'll pop up soon to take a breather.

   And, if you're very quiet,

You'll glimpse him then:

     Small but, nonetheless, a wonder.

ISABEL JOSHLIN GLASER

CAMEL

Tan
leather seats;
optional fur.
Sun roof. Runs on no gas. Stalls
seldom. Steers
with a whispered command to the ears.
Has four-leg drive. Hauls
anything: travelers, sleeping bags, frankincense, myrrh.
Overheats
never. An efficient sedan
is this passenger mammal.

SYLVIA CASSEDY

SMALL, SMALLER

I thought that I knew all there was to know
Of being small, until I saw once, black against the snow,
A shrew, trapped in my footprint, jump and fall
And jump again and fall, the hole too deep, the walls too tall.

RUSSELL HOBAN

THE CHIPMUNK'S DAY

In and out the bushes, up the ivy,
Into the hole
By the old oak stump, the chipmunk flashes.
Up the pole

To the feeder full of seeds he dashes,
Stuffs his cheeks,
The chickadee and titmouse scold him.
Down he streaks.

Red as the leaves the wind blows off the maple,
Red as a fox,
Striped like a skunk, the chipmunk whistles
Past the love seat, past the mailbox,

Down the path,
Home to his warm hole stuffed with sweet
Things to eat.
Neat and slight and shining, his front feet

Curled at his breast, he sits there while the sun
Stripes the red west
With its last light: the chipmunk
Dives to his rest.

RANDALL JARRELL

SQUIRREL

Scolding
Holding
Boldly raiding
Plotting
Waiting
Ambuscading
Highly climbing
And descending
Digging
Hiding
And forgetting.

FELICE HOLMAN

THE MOUSE

I heard a mouse
Bitterly complaining
In a crack of moonlight
Aslant on the floor—

"Little I ask
And that little is not granted.
There are few crumbs
In this world anymore.

"The breadbox is tin
And I cannot get in.

"The jam's in a jar
My teeth cannot mar.

"The cheese sits by itself
On the pantry shelf.

"All night I run
Searching and seeking,
All night I run
About on the floor,

"Moonlight is there
And a bare place for dancing,
But no little feast
Is spread anymore."

ELIZABETH COATSWORTH

MOUSE AT NIGHT

Never a sound in the dark
    But the little gray mouse will hear,
Never a sound in the night
    But he feels the paw of fear.

The turn of a key in the lock,
    The tread of feet on the stair,
And the little gray mouse must hide away
    Lest danger be creeping there.

But when a stillness fills the house,
    And the dark is thickly laid,
The little gray mouse goes round about
    Busy and unafraid.

LELAND B. JACOBS

61

BAT

All day bats drowse in houses' eaves
    Like tents collapsed for storage,
But when dusk darkens, like fall leaves,
    They loosen. Then they forage

For juicy June bugs, meaty moths,
    Mosquitoes (eaten rare).
They're scary. But there's nothing like
    A bat to clear the air.

X. J. KENNEDY

THE BAT

By day the bat is cousin to the mouse.
He likes the attic of an aging house.

His fingers make a hat about his head.
His pulse beat is so slow we think him dead.

He loops in crazy figures half the night
Among the trees that face the corner light.

But when he brushes up against a screen,
We are afraid of what our eyes have seen:

For something is amiss or out of place
When mice with wings can wear a human face.

THEODORE ROETHKE

63

JANUARY DEER

I am a January deer,
so swift and light
the hardpacked snow does not even
    crunch
beneath my hooves.
While others around me
sleep in silent caves,
    I run
through the white world
    with wide-open eyes.

MARILYN SINGER

DEER

Beautiful deer!
sleep in the grass
    making deer-beds of silk
among black-eyed Susans, milkweed
    and Queen Anne's lace.

When the snow melts
    we come to see
grass pressed down in the
    shape of deer.

Tan like ginger, fawns,
    snowdrops on their backs,
hunt for salt in winter,
    in summer
apples and bark.

    Graceful deer
run through the fields,
    do not tire till dawn.

ALIKI BARNSTONE

REINDEER

When icicles hang from the trees
And the north wind whips our sides,
When berries fall on the frozen pond,
The reindeer takes great strides.
He crosses winter snow and ice,
He leaps the frozen park;
At night he rides the frosty sky
And gallops through the dark.

SYLVIA READ

65

THE HORSE

The horse moves
independently
without reference
to his load

He has eyes
like a woman and
turns them
about, throws

back his ears
and is generally
conscious of
the world. Yet

he pulls when
he must and
pulls well, blowing
fog from

his nostrils
like fumes from
the twin
exhausts of a car.

WILLIAM CARLOS WILLIAMS

FOAL

Come trotting up
Beside your mother,
Little skinny.

Lay your neck across
Her back, and whinny,
Little foal.

You think you're a horse
Because you can trot—
But you're not.

Your eyes are so wild,
And each leg is as tall
As a pole;

And you're only a skittish
Child, after all,
Little foal.

MARY BRITTON MILLER

MARE

When the mare shows you
her yellow teeth, stuck
with clover and gnawed leaf,
you know they have combed
pastures of spiky grasses,
and tough thickets.

But when you offer her
a sweet, white lump
from the trembling plate
of your palm—she trots
to the gate, sniffs—
and takes it with velvet lips.

JUDITH THURMAN

A HORSE IS A HORSE

I would like to be
A horse wild and free
Galloping with flying mane
Over miles of wide field,
Leaping fences and walls,
With the whistle of wind-sound
So strong in my ears
    That I
    Can simply not
    Certainly
    Not possibly
    Hear
        When anyone
            Calls.

DOROTHY W. BARUCH

OLD HORSE

He's worked out
like a lead-mine, gray
dusty deserted,
lost for metal hammering metal,
clatter of feet and gear.

Head hung over a gate,
lower lip drooped
disconsolate,
he stands unmoving.
Then suddenly flings his mane
whipping a gauze of flies
that suck the juices
round suppurating eyes.

No one comes
to lead him to the stable, feed him oats
and polish his flanks to silver.
Lead-gray, weight
carried on three legs,
he sags with the sodden day
wrong side of the gate.

PHOEBE HESKETH

67

ZEBRA

The eagle's shadow runs across the plain,
Towards the distant, nameless, air-blue mountains.
But the shadows of the round young Zebra
Sit close between their delicate hoofs all day,
    where they stand immovable,
And wait for the evening, wait to stretch out, blue,
Upon a plain, painted brick-red by the sunset,
And to wander to the waterhole.

ISAK DINESEN

HIPPOPOTAMUS

The Hippopotamus—Hippo for short—
Is as lazy as sin, it is sad to report.
He wallows for hours up to his eyes
In mud while tropical Butterflies
Flicker above him through the skies,
While Peacocks scream and Apes cavort.
Black water trickles down from his ears,
Around his head the blue mist clears;
He lifts his broad back, shakes off flies,
Opens his pink mouth, blinks his eyes,
Then sinks back under, and disappears.

WILLIAM JAY SMITH

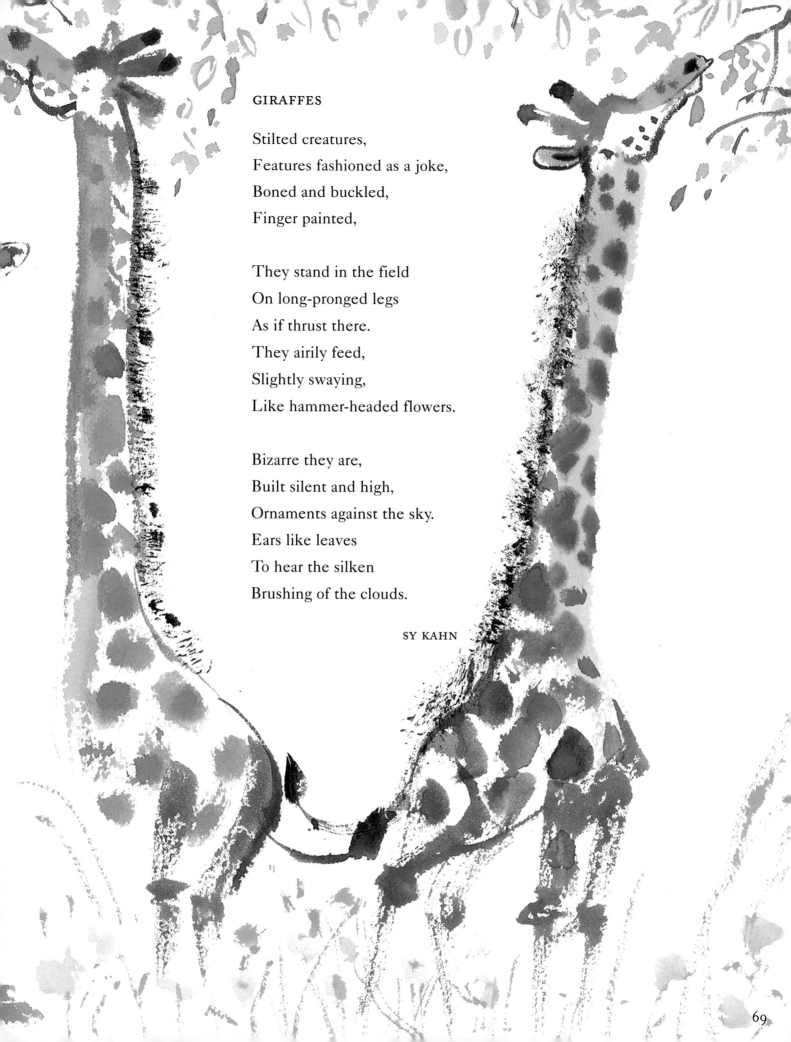

GIRAFFES

Stilted creatures,
Features fashioned as a joke,
Boned and buckled,
Finger painted,

They stand in the field
On long-pronged legs
As if thrust there.
They airily feed,
Slightly swaying,
Like hammer-headed flowers.

Bizarre they are,
Built silent and high,
Ornaments against the sky.
Ears like leaves
To hear the silken
Brushing of the clouds.

SY KAHN

RHINOCEROS

When the rhinoceros
Feeling nasty
Turns and runs
Slowly and then faster
Like a rolling
Boulder after
His foe and
Butts him with
The thick spike
On his nose,

It's no help
To know that
His hard horn
Is only made
Of hair, like
The flared mane
Of a lion,
Or the horse's
Airy tail
That flicks and flows.

VALERIE WORTH

RHINOCEROS

There is no rush.
I have slept away
centuries of midday sun,
brushed folded skin
through canes and banyan,
hoof-toed through still grass
with eyes half-closed
to the healing mud
of ancient swamps.
Centuries are mapped on my forehead;
I am not of this time.
My horn beckons…

JUDITH NICHOLLS

ELEPHANTS PLODDING

Plod! Plod!
And what ages of time
the worn arches of their spines support!

D. H. LAWRENCE

ELEPHANTS MUNCHING

Elephants munching
    on grass—loving
Heads side by side.

JACK KEROUAC

TURN, TURN, TURN

There is a time for considering elephants
There is no time for not considering elephants

ADRIAN MITCHELL

I AM LYNX

I am Lynx.
I pad softly through deep grass,
crouch, with muscles bunched—
                        and *pounce*.
Paws shoot sharp claws, and mouse
cannot escape
                        this time.
But then I hear a branch snap. My ears
swivel. I crouch again. Through the blades,
the man stands. I gaze into the sun-glow,
low and blood-red behind him.
I am not afraid, just cautious.
I wait. The river mumbles
and mutters in the distance.
Then I ripple like wind through the grass—
half a mouse dangling—toward the dark woods.
I am quiet as the approaching night.

JONATHAN LONDON

LEOPARDS

While monkeys nod
And birds are still,
Hushed the forest,
Hushed the hill,

A leap of leopards
Princely prowls,
Hunting where
The jackal howls.

PAULINE CLARKE

CHEETAH

A cheetah has metal girder teeth
it goes hurling down through the jungle
throwing out its fear

DARREN COYLES

LION

The name opens wide
as soon as you
speak it   L I
O N   Jaw unhinges
teeth flash white
sharp   against all that
red

From all the best possible
choices   FLEA   TOAD
PEACOCK   he picked this
for himself   LION
the only one he could say
while   ROARING!

BARBARA JUSTER ESBENSEN

THE TIGER

In the immensity of the jungle
the orange tiger lives.
Silently he moves
and gives
the soft sound of his padded feet
back to the silent night.
The hot wind blows,
the treetops bend
and sway beneath the cloud gray sky.
And where the water spills
cold from the distant hills,
he crouches low to drink.

JOAN E. CASS

WOLF

The Iron Wolf, the Iron Wolf

Stands on the world with jagged fur.
The rusty Moon rolls through the sky.
The iron river cannot stir.
The iron wind leaks out a cry

Caught in the barbed and iron wood.
The Iron Wolf runs over the snow
Looking for a speck of blood.
Only the Iron Wolf shall know

The iron of his fate.
He lifts his nose and moans,
Licks the world clean as a plate
And leaves his own bones.

TED HUGHES

WOLF

Mine is the howl
that chills the spine
in the forest gloom;
mine is the whine.

Mine is the nose
that breathes in fear
when danger's close;
mine is the ear.

Mine is the fur
the huntsmen trade;
mine is the fur,
I am afraid.

JUDITH NICHOLLS

FOX

Down from the mountains
Into camp,
The air was cold,
Earth lay damp,
Came a silver fox.
Slyly, she'd say:
    "They all will sleep till the stars slip away."

On delicate feet
She drifted like smoke,
From trees
To cot,
From cot
To coals.
The fire drowsed.
Smiling, she'd say:
    "All will sleep till the stars slip away."

Ears stood pricked,
Her warm breath curled,
She tasted air,
Yet the wildness in her
Never sensed,
With quick eyes
Or cautious paws,
How I watched her:
    Till she slipped away with the stars.

DEBORAH CHANDRA

THE SPUN GOLD FOX

Sing in the silver fog of night,
Voice of foxhound, bellow-bright,
Sing me the silver song of fox,
Wary and watching the moon-dipped rocks.
Quivering nostril, lifted paw,
Sniffing the mist for the smell of dog.
Sing me foxhound, lemon-white,
Sing me the song of a fox tonight.
Bay me the story, old, old, old,
Of a fox that runs and a moon that's cold;
In the valley, the hill, near
    the speckled rocks,
Bay me the run of the spun gold fox.

PATRICIA HUBBELL

RED FOX AT DAWN

The fox glides like a flame through frozen fields of morning,
On black velvet feet.
His jet-black pointed ears prick up as he hears
The first cocks crow on far off farms.
He pauses, listening,
Then yawns a delicate yawn and licks his chops
And swiftly flows into the glowing dawn,
Passing like a comet out of sight,
Trailing his tail—a plume of firelight—
As bright tongues lick across the morning sky,
And all the frosted grass bursts into life
With rubies, garnets, diamonds sparkling.
The red fox slips across red jeweled fields,
On feet of night.

DAHLOV IPCAR

77

SKUNK

Skunk's footfall plods padded
    But like the thunder-crash
He makes the night woods nervous
    And wears the lightning-flash—

From nose to tail a zigzag spark
    As warning to us all
That thunderbolts are very like
    The strokes he can let fall.

That cloudburst soak, that dazzling bang
    Of stink he can let drop
Over you like a cloak of tar
    Will bring you to a stop.

O Skunk! O King of Stinkards!
    Only the Moon knows
You are her prettiest, ugliest flower,
    Her blackest, whitest rose!

TED HUGHES

OTTER

Sun-flickery
in his coat of many bubbles
he melts into water,
seldom troubles to rise for air,
an oil-slickery streak
of brilliantine, there
below the surface:
a shimmer below the glimmer
and spangle of summer,
a swirl with a tail,
a stain, a shadow
oil-slickery in his trickery
of dodges and feints
and dives and bubbly delvings.

Yet in the field all yikkery
he lolloped, less than a dog
lay like a rough old log
in the sun, dry as a stick;
and I ached to toss him in the pool,
to see him wed to water,
doing his sleekings, slick,
to his own satisfaction
in dark liquefaction.

BRIAN CARTER

78

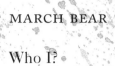

MARCH BEAR

Who I?
   Where I?
When I now?
   No matter
Need water
Few berries
Fresh ants
   Not so hungry
Or am I?
Don't think so
   Not yet
And anyway it's too early for honey
Funny
That odor
   This river
That hollow
   This den
I know them
   Well, sort of
I've been here
   But when?
   No matter
New morning
Remember it then

MARILYN SINGER

THE SMALL BROWN BEAR

The small brown bear
fishes
with stony paws

eating ice salmon
all waterfall slippery
till his teeth ache.

MICHAEL BALDWIN

79

THE SLOTH

In moving slow he has no Peer.
You ask him something in his Ear,
He thinks about it for a Year;

And, then, before he says a Word
There, upside down (unlike a Bird),
He will assume that you have Heard—

A most Ex-as-per-at-ing Lug.
But should you call his manner Smug,
He'll sigh and give his Branch a Hug;

Then off again to Sleep he goes,
Still swaying gently by his Toes,
And you just *know* he knows he knows.

THEODORE ROETHKE

RACCOON

Raccoon,
with your black ringed eyes
and tiny paws,
startled at your work,
to you my garbage can
is full
of treasure.

CHARLOTTE ZOLOTOW

ANTEATER

Imagine overturning
The teeming anthill
Without a qualm,
Calmly sweeping
Up its angry
Inhabitants on a
Long sticky tongue,
And swallowing the
Lot with relish—
As if those
Beady little bodies
Made just so many
Mouthfuls of red
Or black caviar.

VALERIE WORTH

OX

The Ox is an honest beast
    who once pulled the plow.
Today the engine reaps and sows.
    What does the Ox do now?

The Ox stands silently beside
    fields that the tractor turns
and for the plowman's hand and voice
    fiercely the dumb Ox yearns.

GEORGE BARKER

CATTLE

How cool the cattle seem!
They love to swish their tails and stand
    Knee-deep within the stream.

BANKO

SHELTER

Her hooves
sinking into
the snow-soaked meadow, she
moves heavily toward sheltering
aspen....

Among
shivering leaves
she waits, smelling the wind,
her head turned slightly as if she
listens....

At dawn
a newborn calf
follows closely at her
side, his small hooves denting the wet
prairie.

ALICE SCHERTLE

MILK-WHITE MOON, PUT THE COWS TO SLEEP

Milk-white moon, put the cows to sleep.
Since five o'clock in the morning,
Since they stood up out of the grass,
Where they slept on their knees and hocks,
They have eaten grass and given their milk
And eaten grass again and given milk,
And kept their heads and teeth at the earth's face.
  Now they are looking at you, milk-white moon.
  Carelessly as they look at the level landscapes,
  Carelessly as they look at a pail of new white milk,
  They are looking at you, wondering not at all, at all,
  If the moon is the skim face top of a pail of milk,
  Wondering not at all, carelessly looking.
  Put the cows to sleep, milk-white moon,
  Put the cows to sleep.

CARL SANDBURG

SEAL

See how he dives
 From the rocks with a zoom!
See how he darts
 Through his watery room
 Past crabs and eels
 And green seaweed,
 Past fluffs of sandy
 Minnow feed!
See how he swims
 With a swerve and a twist,
A flip of the flipper,
A flick of the wrist!
Quicksilver-quick,
 Softer than spray,
Down he plunges
And sweeps away;
Before you can think,
Before you can utter
Words like "Dill pickle"
Or "Apple butter,"
Back up he swims
 Past Sting Ray and Shark,
Out with a zoom,
 A whoop, a bark;
Before you can say
 Whatever you wish,
 He plops at your side
 With a mouthful of fish!

WILLIAM JAY SMITH

84

POLAR BEAR

White are the snows upon the sea,
The frozen sea, and white the wind
Blowing through corridors of cold,
Through solitary spheres of night.
By cliff of blue and frozen sea
Roaming a chilly pasture where
Meadows are green in fields of ice,
In white fleece walks the polar bear.

SYLVIA READ

85

CAT IN MOONLIGHT

Through moonlight's milk
She slowly passes
As soft as silk
Between tall grasses.
I watch her go
So sleek and white,
As white as snow,
The moon so bright
I hardly know
White moon, white fur,
Which is the light
And which is her.

DOUGLAS GIBSON

POEM

As the cat
climbed over
the top of

the jamcloset
first the right
forefoot

carefully
then the hind
stepped down

into the pit of
the empty
flowerpot.

WILLIAM CARLOS WILLIAMS

CHESHIRE DAWN

They pounced on me
And there they sat,
The purring sun
And the rising cat.
And it stayed with me
As the day wore on,
The indelible smile
Of Cheshire Dawn.

VICTORIA FORRESTER

PUSSY CAT

A pussy cat with yellow eyes
    That purrs and dozes,
She is intelligent and wise,
A pussy cat with yellow eyes,
She cannot talk and never tries,
    As one supposes—
A pussy cat with yellow eyes
    That purrs and dozes.

TOM ROBINSON

THE STRAY CAT

It's just an old alley cat
that has followed us all the way home.

It hasn't a star on its forehead,
or a silky satiny coat.

No proud tiger stripes, no dainty tread,
no elegant velvet throat.

It's a splotchy, blotchy
city cat, not pretty cat,
a rough little tough little bag of old bones.

"Beauty," we shall call you.
"Beauty, come in."

EVE MERRIAM

ALLEY CAT

A bit of jungle in the street
He goes on velvet toes,
And slinking through the shadows, stalks
Imaginary foes.

ESTHER VALCK GEORGES

CAT ON THE LEDGE

Nonchalant cat
Treading the sill
Importantly fat;

Unflurried where
Dizziness reels
High in the air;

Nonchalant puss,
Picking your way
Quite without fuss

On the sheer edge
Crazily high
Of the bright ledge;

Choosing your spot
Warm in the sun,
Nor caring a jot

For frenzy and roar
Of traffic below;
You can ignore

Trifles like that,
And doze off to dreams,
Somnolent cat!

LYDIA PENDER

THE DOLLAR DOG

I had a dollar dog named Spot.
He wasn't much, but he was a lot
Of *kinds* of dog, plus a few parts flea,
Seven parts yapper, and seventy-three
Or seventy-four parts this-and-that.
The only thing he wasn't was cat.
He was collie-terrier-spaniel-hound
And everything else they have at the pound.
Yes, some might call him a mongrel, but
To me he was thoroughbred, pedigreed mutt.
A middle-sized nothing, or slightly smaller,
But a lot of kinds to get for a dollar.

JOHN CIARDI

PUPPY

Catch and shake the cobra garden hose.
Scramble on panicky paws and flee
The hiss of tensing nozzle nose,
Or stalk that snobbish bee.

The backyard world is vast as park
With belly-tickle grass and stun
Of sudden sprinkler squalls that arc
Rainbows to the yap yap sun.

ROBERT L. TYLER

OUR DOG CHASING SWIFTS

A border collie has been bred to keep
Order among those wayward bleaters, sheep.
Ours, in a sheepless garden, vainly tries
To herd the screaming black sheep of the skies.

U. A. FANTHORPE

SWIMMER

Wading out of streams and lakes
His wet coat plastered down, he takes
A gulp of water now and then,
Watches a gull, wades on again,
Leaves behind a silver trail
Of drops from off his ears and tail—
On shore he plants his feet and shakes.

DOROTHY ALDIS

THE BLOODHOUND

I am the dog world's best detective.
My sleuthing nose is so effective
I sniff the guilty at a distance
And then they lead a doomed existence.
My well-known record for convictions
Has earned me lots of maledictions
From those whose trail of crime I scented
And sent to prison, unlamented.
Folks either must avoid temptation
Or face my nasal accusation.

EDWARD ANTHONY

DACHSHUND

Sharp nose raised,
He centipedes by,
Three dogs long…
And half-a-dog high—

A round, smooth hull
For his tail to steer,
And two little squat legs
Bringing up the rear.

CLIVE SANSOM

A BEAGLE SPEAKS OF NOSES

I should be good.
I wish I could.
But
I sniff and sniff.
I catch a whiff
of something new
or old to chew.
What can it be?
My nose drags me
so I drag you.
What can I do
but wind through weeds
and twine through trees,
check at each pole,
inspect each hole?
Please don't be cross.
My nose is boss.

TONY JOHNSTON

THE MONKEY

Mischievous monkey; behavior cantankerous,
Raucous and crude, argumentative, rancorous,
Crafty, deceitful, activities prankerous,
Grabber of food, and you don't even thankerous.

Mischievous monkey, what *are* we to do?
You don't like *us*, and we *sure* don't like *you!*

ROBERT S. OLIVER

THE MANDRILL

In the Mandrill
unrefined
Beauty and Beast
are well combined.
How would *you* like
to have that face
to look at in your looking-glass?
And all the other
jungle creatures
what must *they* think
of those strange features?
And that odd name
the Mandrill—can
it be he hopes
to BE a *man?*
But *that* face
won't
wash
off
with
soap:
I fear poor Mandrill
has
no
hope.

CONRAD AIKEN

IMPASSE

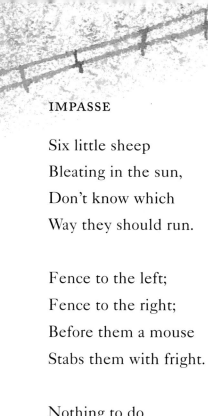

Six little sheep
Bleating in the sun,
Don't know which
Way they should run.

Fence to the left;
Fence to the right;
Before them a mouse
Stabs them with fright.

Nothing to do
But to wheel and go—
A little too much
For sheep to know.

LEW SARETT

APRIL

The little goat
crops
new grass lying down
leaps up eight inches
into air and
lands on four feet.
Not a tremor—
solid in the
spring and serious
he walks away.

YVOR WINTERS

WHALES WEEP NOT!

All the whales in the wider deeps, hot are they, as they urge
on and on, and dive beneath the icebergs.
The right whales, the sperm-whales, the hammer-heads,
　　the killers
there they blow, there they blow, hot wild white breath out
　　of the sea!

D. H. LAWRENCE

THE WHALES

　　There Leviathan
Hugest of living creatures, on the deep
Stretched like a promontory, sleeps or swims,
And seems a moving land, and at his gills
Draws in, and at his trunk spouts out, a sea.

JOHN MILTON

WHALE

An evenly balanced
word   W H A L E
it floats lazily on the page
or dives straight down
to the bottom and beyond
all breath held   held
held   then whoooosh!
The   A   blows its top
into the sun!   W H A L E
serene
sings to us   wet
green sounds from the deepest
part of the alphabet

BARBARA JUSTER ESBENSEN

94

THE WHALE GHOST

When we've emptied
the sea of the
last great
whale

will he come
rising
from a deep remembered
dive

sending from his
blowhole
a ghostly fog
of spout?

Will he call
with haunting cry

to his herd that
rode the
seas with joyous
ease,

to the whale that swam
beside him,

to the calf?

Will we hear his
sad song
echoing
over the water?

LILIAN MOORE

INDEX OF TITLES

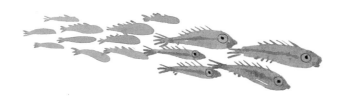

INDEX OF AUTHORS

ACKNOWLEDGMENTS

Grateful acknowledgment is made to the following for permission to reprint previously published material:

The Estate of Valerie Worth Bahlke for "Rhinoceros" and "Wasp" by Valerie Worth Bahlke. Both copyright © 1994 by George W. Bahlke. Reprinted by permission of George W. Bahlke, Executor of the Estate.

Zoë Bailey for "Ant" from *Noah's Ark*, compiled by Michael Harrison and Christopher Stuart-Clark (Oxford University Press, 1983). Reprinted by permission of Zoë Bailey.

Rebecca Jean Baker for "I Catch a Firefly" by Rebecca Caudill from *Come Along* (Holt, Rinehart & Winston, 1969). Copyright © 1969 by Rebecca Caudill. Reprinted by permission of Rebecca Jean Baker.

Michael Baldwin for "The Small Brown Bear" from *A First Poetry Book*, compiled by John L. Foster (Oxford University Press, 1980). Copyright © 1979 by Michael Baldwin. Reprinted by permission of Michael Baldwin.

Bantam Doubleday Dell Publishing Group, Inc., for "The Bat" copyright © 1938 by Theodore Roethke, "The Heron" copyright © 1937 by Theodore Roethke, and "The Sloth" copyright © 1950 by Theodore Roethke from *The Collected Poems of Theodore Roethke*. "The Tree Toads" by Rachel Field from *Taxis and Toadstools*. Reprinted by permission of Doubleday, a division of Bantam Doubleday Dell Publishing Group, Inc.

The Estate of the late George Barker and Faber & Faber Ltd. for "Ox" and "Snake" by George Barker from *The Alphabetical Zoo*. Reprinted by permission of A M Heath & Company and the Estate of George Barker.

Boyds Mills Press for "Oh, to Be an Earthworm" by Lillian Morrison from *Whistling the Morning In*. Copyright © 1992 by Lillian Morrison. Reprinted by permission of Wordsong, Boyds Mills Press. "Caterpillars" by Brod Bagert from *If Only I Could Fly* (Boyds Mills Press, 1984). Reprinted by permission of Boyds Mills Press.

BPI Communications for "The Bloodhound" by Edward Anthony from *Every Dog Has His Say* (Watson-Guptil, 1947). Reprinted by permission of Watson-Guptil Publications, a division of BPI Communications.

Curtis Brown Group Ltd. for "Leopards" and "Peacocks" by Pauline Clarke from *Silver Bells & Cockle Shells*. Copyright © 1962 by Pauline Clarke. "Love Song for a Jellyfish" by Sandra Hochman from *Earthworks*, 1967. Copyright © 1960 by Sandra Hochman. "I'm a Parrot" and "Crab Dance" by Grace Nichols from *Come On into My Tropical Garden*. Copyright © 1988 by Grace Nichols. "Alligator" by Maxine Kumin from *No One Writes a Letter to the Snail* (G.P. Putnam's Sons). Copyright © 1962 by Maxine Kumin. Reprinted by permission of Curtis Brown Group Ltd.

Brian Carter for "Otter" from *Poetry Plus*, compiled by Marney, Ashton & Parle (Schofield & Sims Ltd., 1982). Reprinted by permission of Brian Carter.

Joan E. Cass for "The Tiger" from *The Hippopotamus' Birthday*, compiled by Linda Jennings (Hodder & Stoughton, 1987). Reprinted by kind permission of Joan E. Cass.

City Lights Books for "Elephants Munching" by Jack Kerouac from *The Dog Writes on the Window with His Nose*, compiled by David Kherkian (Four Winds Press). Copyright © 1970, 1971 by the Estate of Jack Kerouac. Reprinted by permission of City Lights Books.

Pie Corbett for "Owl" from *Another Third Poetry Book*, compiled by John L. Foster (Oxford University Press, 1988). Copyright © 1988 by Pie Corbett. Reprinted by permission of Pie Corbett.

Dundurn Press Ltd. for "To a Monarch Butterfly" by Lola Sneyd from *The Concrete Giraffe* (Simon & Pierre Publishing Company, Ltd.). Copyright © 1984 by Lola Sneyd. Reprinted by permission of Dundurn Press Ltd.

Faber & Faber Ltd. for "Trout" by Seamus Heaney from *Death of a Naturalist*. "Rhinoceros," "Song-Thrush," and "Wolf" by Judith Nicholls from *Dragonsfire*. Reprinted by permission of Faber & Faber Ltd.

U. A. Fanthorpe for "Our Dog Chasing Swifts" from *The Oxford Treasury of Children's Poems*, compiled by Michael Harrison and Christopher Stuart-Clark (Oxford University Press, 1988). Reprinted by permission of U. A. Fanthorpe.

Farrar, Straus & Giroux, Inc., for "The Mole" by Jeanne Steig from *Consider the Lemming*. Copyright © 1988 by Jeanne Steig. "Mosquito" and "Sparrow" by Valerie Worth from *More Small Poems*. Copyright © 1976 by Valerie Worth. "Anteater" and "Octopus" by Valerie Worth from *Small Poems Again*. Copyright © 1986 by Valerie Worth. "Hippopotamus" and "Seal" by William Jay Smith from *Laughing Time*. Copyright © 1990 by William Jay Smith. "Rich Lizard" and "Fox" by Deborah Chandra from *Rich Lizard*. Copyright © 1993 by Deborah Chandra. Reprinted by permission of Farrar, Straus & Giroux, Inc.

Aileen Fisher for "Frogs in Spring" from *Out in the Dark and Daylight* (Harper & Row, 1980). "Bluebird" by Aileen Fisher, from *In the Woods, in the Meadow, in the Sky* (Charles Scribner's Sons, 1965). Reprinted by permission of Aileen Fisher, who controls all rights.

Mrs. Dorothy Gibson for "Cat in Moonlight" by Douglas Gibson from *Happy Landing*, by Douglas Gibson (Bell & Hyman, 1971). Also printed in *Cats Are Cats*, compiled by Nancy Larrick (Philomel Books, 1988). Reprinted by permission of Mrs. Dorothy Gibson.

Isabel Joshlin Glaser for "About Muskrat, Let's Say...." Copyright by Isabel Joshlin Glaser. Reprinted by permission of Isabel Joshlin Glaser, who controls all rights.

Golden Quill Press for "Puppy" by Robert L. Tyler from *The Deposition of Don Quixote and Other Poems*, compiled by Robert L. Tyler. Also printed in *Reflections on a Gift of Watermelon Pickle and Other Modern Verse*, edited by Stephen Dunning et al. (Lothrop, 1966). Reprinted by permission of Golden Quill Press.

James W. Hackett for "A Bitter Morning," "The Earthworm Wriggles," "Ladybug," and "The Grasshopper Springs" from *The Zen Haiku and Other Zen Poems of J. W. Hackett* (Japan Publications, Inc., 1983). Copyright © 1983 by James W. Hackett. Distributed in the U.S.A. by Zen View Distributors, P.O. Box 313, La Honda, CA 94020-0313. Reprinted by permission of James W. Hackett.

Harcourt Brace & Company for "Splinter" and "Milk-White Moon, Put